Level 4 is ideal for ch
longer stories with a wi
to start reading indeper

CW00926874

Special features:

Clear type

Full,
exciting
story

Richer,
more varied
vocabulary

Peter and his grandfather lived
next to a beautiful meadow.

Next to the meadow, there was
a dark forest. And in the middle
of the forest, there lived a
hungry wolf.

6

7

Longer
sentences

Detailed
illustrations
to capture the
imagination

"Stay in the garden, Peter," said
Grandfather. "Never go into the
meadow on your own."

"But why not?" said Peter.

"There is a hungry wolf in the
dark forest," said Grandfather.
"He could come creeping into the
meadow and eat you up!"

8

9

Educational Consultant: Geraldine Taylor

Book Banding Consultant: Kate Ruttle

LADYBIRD BOOKS

UK | USA | Canada | Ireland | Australia
India | New Zealand | South Africa

Ladybird Books is part of the Penguin Random House group of companies
whose addresses can be found at global.penguinrandomhouse.com.

ladybird.com

Penguin
Random House
UK

First published 2015
008

Copyright © Ladybird Books Ltd, 2015

Ladybird, Read it yourself and the Ladybird logo are registered or
unregistered trademarks owned by Ladybird Books Ltd

The moral right of the illustrator has been asserted

Printed in China

A CIP catalogue record for this book is available from the British Library

ISBN: 978-0-723-28068-2

Peter
and the Wolf

Illustrated by Milly Teggle

Peter and his grandfather lived next to a beautiful meadow.

Next to the meadow, there was a dark forest. And in the middle of the forest, there lived a hungry wolf.

"Stay in the garden, Peter," said Grandfather. "Never go into the meadow on your own."

"But why not?" said Peter.

"There is a hungry wolf in the dark forest," said Grandfather. "He could come creeping into the meadow and eat you up!"

9

Peter looked over the garden wall.
The meadow looked very beautiful.

A little red bird flew up to a big
tree. "Peter!" called the bird.
"Why don't you come and play
in the meadow?"

Peter climbed over the garden wall
and went into the meadow.

There was a pond in the middle
of the meadow.

A duck waddled past Peter,
then she jumped into the pond
and swam away.

The little red bird flew down to the duck.

"Come back!" she said to the duck. "What a funny walk! Why don't you fly like me?"

"I don't want to fly like you," said the duck. "Why don't you swim like me?"

The two birds were very cross
with one another, and they made
a lot of noise.

Suddenly, Peter saw a cat come
creeping towards the birds.
"Look out!" called Peter.
"The cat will catch you!"

At once, the little red bird
flew up to the top of the big
tree and the duck swam to
the middle of the pond.

Just then, Peter's grandfather
came into the garden.

He looked over the wall and
saw Peter in the meadow.
He was very cross with him.

"Come back at once, Peter!"
said Grandfather.

So Peter climbed over the wall
and went back into the garden
with his grandfather.

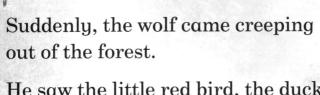

Suddenly, the wolf came creeping out of the forest.

He saw the little red bird, the duck and the cat. He was so hungry that he wanted to eat them all.

The cat climbed to the very top of the tree, where the little red bird was sitting.

The two of them waited to see what would happen next.

The frightened duck jumped out of the pond! She waddled off as fast as she could. But the hungry wolf ran faster and caught her in his big mouth!

Then the wolf walked round
and round the tree where the cat
and the little red bird were sitting.

The hungry wolf looked up at
them. They were very frightened.

Peter found a very long rope and climbed on top of the garden wall.

"Fly around the wolf's head!" he called out to the little red bird. "Make him dizzy! But stay away from his big mouth!"

33

The little red bird flew round and round the wolf's head. The hungry wolf tried to catch the little red bird, but after a time he was very dizzy.

Peter climbed up the big tree.
Then he let the rope down and
caught the wolf by the tail.
The wolf jumped up and down
and tried to get away.
But Peter held on to the rope.

Just then, Grandfather saw Peter
sitting in the tree.

"What are you doing up there?"
he called.

"I've got the wolf by the tail,"
said Peter. "Look!"

Suddenly, hunters came into
the meadow, looking for the wolf.

"Here he is," said Peter.
"Take him away!"

The hunters took the wolf
to another forest, a very
long way away from Peter
and his grandfather, the cat,
and the little red bird.

So Peter's grandfather then let him play in the beautiful meadow, with the little red bird and the cat.

45

How much do you remember about the story of Peter and the Wolf? Answer these questions and find out!

- Who does Peter live with?

- Who lives in the dark forest?

- What is in the middle of the meadow?

- What does Peter say the cat will do to the birds?

- How does Peter catch the wolf?

- Who takes the wolf away?